Dear Parent:
Your child's love of reading starts here!

Every child learns to read in a different way and at his or her own speed. You can help your young reader improve and become more confident by encouraging his or her own interests and abilities. You can also guide your child's spiritual development by reading stories with biblical values and Bible stories, like I Can Read! books published by Zonderkidz. From books your child reads with you to the first books he or she reads alone, there are I Can Read! books for every stage of reading:

SHARED READING
Basic language, word repetition, and whimsical illustrations, ideal for sharing with your emergent reader.

BEGINNING READING
Short sentences, familiar words, and simple concepts for children eager to read on their own.

READING WITH HELP
Engaging stories, longer sentences, and language play for developing readers.

READING ALONE
Complex plots, challenging vocabulary, and high-interest topics for the independent reader.

ADVANCED READING
Short paragraphs, chapters, and exciting themes for the perfect bridge to chapter books.

I Can Read! books have introduced children to the joy of reading since 1957. Featuring award-winning authors and illustrators and a fabulous cast of beloved characters, I Can Read! books set the standard for beginning readers.

A lifetime of discovery begins with the magical words **"I Can Read!"**

Visit www.icanread.com for information on enriching your child's reading experience.
Visit www.zonderkidz.com for more Zonderkidz I Can Read! titles.

"Each of you must respect your mother and father"
—*Leviticus 19:3*

ZONDERKIDZ

The Berenstain Bears® Help Their Neighbors
Copyright © 2010 by Berenstain Publishing, Inc.
Illustrations © 2010 by Berenstain Publishing, Inc.

Requests for information should be addressed to:
Zondervan, 5300 Patterson Ave SE, Grand Rapids, Michigan 49530

ISBN 978-0-310-72164-2 (hardcover)

Honey Hunt Helpers ISBN 9780310721017 (2012)
Mama's Helpers ISBN 9780310720997 (2011)
Help the Homeless ISBN 9780310721024 (2012)

Editor: Mary Hassinger
Art direction: Diane Mielke

Printed in China

13 14 15 16 17 18 /DSC/ 21 20 19 18 17 16 15 14 13 12 11 10 9 8 7 6 5 4 3 2 1

I Can Read!
BEGINNING 1 READING

The Berenstain Bears
Honey Hunt Helpers

Story and Pictures By
Jan and Mike Berenstain

Living Lights™

GOOD DEED SCOUTS

ZONDERVAN.com/
AUTHORTRACKER
follow your favorite authors

The Good Deed Scouts—Brother, Sister,
Fred, and Lizzy—saw a sign:
"Honey contest today.
Big prize for the best honey."

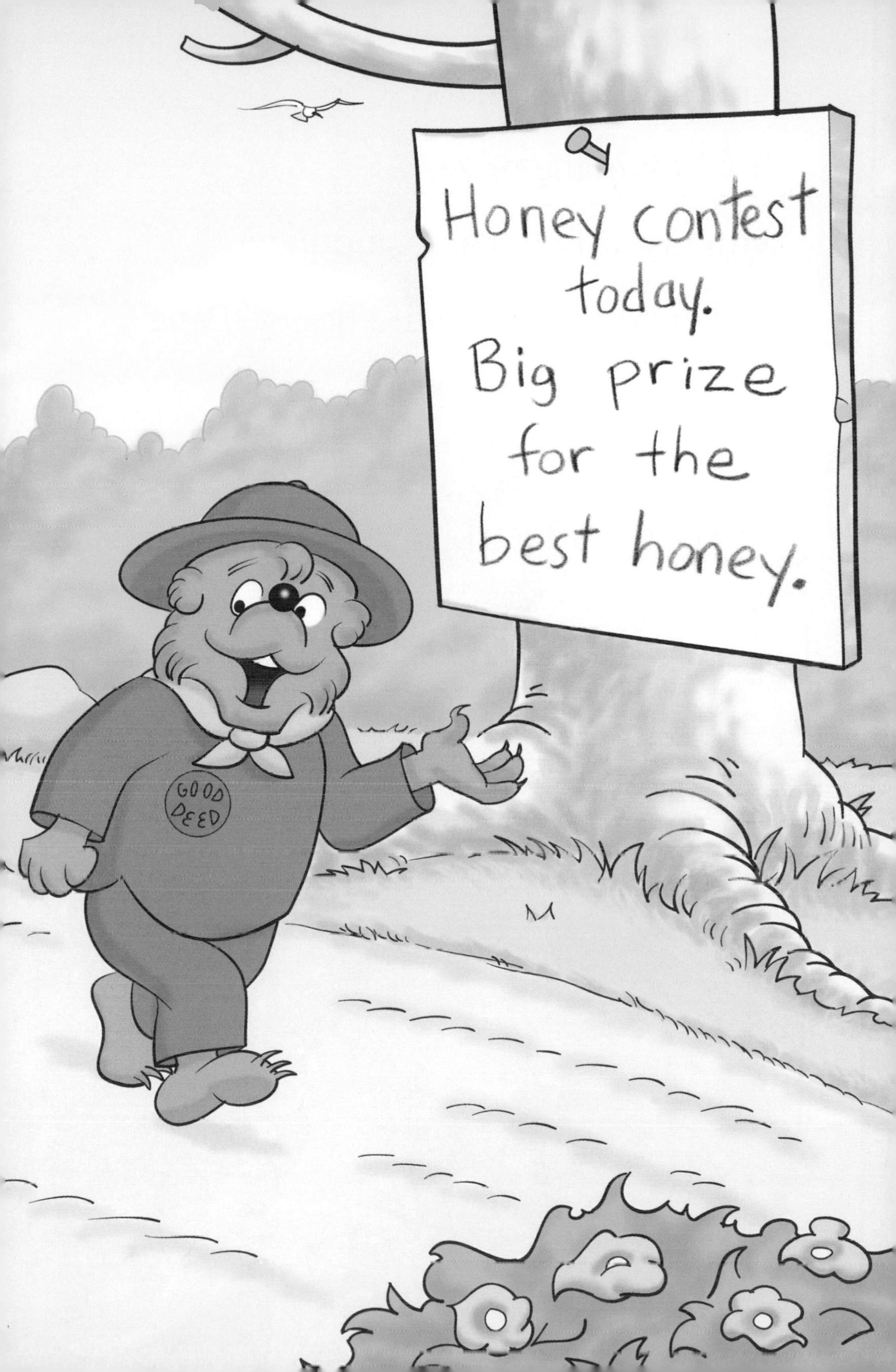
Honey contest today.
Big prize for the best honey.
GOOD DEED

Papa saw the sign too.

"I will win the prize

with my wild honey," said Papa.

"Where do you get wild honey, Papa?"

asked Sister.

"From the wild bee tree," said Papa.

"I am going on a honey hunt."

"We will help you, Papa," said Brother.

"That will be our good deed for the day."

"Thank you," said Papa to the scouts.

"I will show you how to hunt honey."

"As the Bible says," pointed out Fred,

"'A wise son brings joy to his father.'"

"Good point, Fred," said Brother.

"First, we cross this fence," said Papa.

But Papa got caught.

"We will help," said the scouts.

"Thank you," said Papa.

"These fences are higher than they look."

"Now, we find a bee," said Papa.
"He will lead us to the wild bee tree."

Papa could not find a bee.

But a bee found him.

"YEOW!" Papa yelled.

"We will help,"

said the scouts.

"There goes the bee!"

"Thank you," said Papa.

"Bees are hard to find these days."

"Now, we cross this stream," said Papa.

But Papa slipped and fell in … SPLASH!!

"We will help," said the scouts.

"Thank you," said Papa.

"Stones are slipperier than they used to be."

Papa followed the bee across a field.

A bull lived in the field.

"It is hot today!" said Papa.

He took out a red cloth and waved it

in front of his face.

The bull saw the cloth and charged.

"We will help!" yelled Brother. "This way!"

"Thank you," said Papa.

"Bulls are faster than I remember."

Papa followed the bee
through a hollow log.
But he did not fit.

"We will help," said the scouts.

"Thank you," said Papa.
"I guess hollow logs are smaller than before."

Papa followed the bee into Big Bear Bog.

But he sank right in.

"We will help," said the scouts. They got a rope and yanked Papa out.

"Thank you," said Papa. "That bog is boggier than I thought."

Papa followed the bee to the edge of a lake.

The bee flew across the lake.

"There he goes!" said Papa.

"We will help," said Sister.

"We will row you across."

"Thank you," said Papa.

"They made this lake wider, I think."

At last, the bee came to his honey tree.

Papa was happy.

"I can almost taste the wild honey!" Papa said.

"Look at all that honey!" said Papa.

But the bees were very angry.

"Look out!" called the scouts.

"Do not worry!" said Papa.

Papa picked the scouts up and ran.

He was faster than the bees.

He left them far behind.

"Look!" said Papa. "Farmer Ben

is winning the honey prize."

"Yum!" said the scouts. "We love honey."

"As the Bible says," pointed out Fred,

"'What is sweeter than honey?'"

"Good point, Fred," said Brother.

Ben gave them all a taste

of his special honey.

"Thanks for helping me, scouts," said Papa.

"You are welcome, Papa," said Brother.

"We like to help you," said Sister.

"As it says in the Bible," Fred pointed out,

"it is good to 'show respect for the elderly.'"

"Hmmm!" said Papa. "Good point, Fred—

I guess!"

"Give her any help she may need from you, for she has been the benefactor of many people..."
—*Romans 16:2*

The Berenstain Bears
MAMA'S HELPERS

Story and Pictures By
Jan and Mike Berenstain

Living
Lights™

GOOD DEED SCOUTS

ZONDERVAN.com/
AUTHORTRACKER
follow your favorite authors

The Good Deed Scouts were up
bright and early.
They were having breakfast at
the Bear family's tree house.

"What shall our good deed be today?"

asked Scout Lizzy.

Scout Brother had an idea.

"Mama could use some help," he said.

"We will be Mama's helpers today,"

said Scout Sister.

"That will be our good deed."

"As the Bible says," pointed out Scout Fred,

"'honor your father and your mother.'"

"Good point, Fred," said Brother.

"Mama," said Sister,

"the Good Deed Scouts will be

your helpers today."

"That's nice," said Mama. "Start by

clearing the table, please."

"The Good Deed Scouts

at your service!" said the Scouts.

After the table was cleared,

there were other chores to do.

The Good Deed Scouts washed, dried,

and put away the dishes.

They washed the counters.

They swept up crumbs

from the kitchen floor.

"You are doing a good job," said Mama.

"Now let's go to the living room.

These rugs need to be cleaned."

The Scouts took the rugs outside.

They hung them up.

They beat them with a rug beater.

Clouds of dust came out.

46

Papa saw the clouds of dust.

He came to see what was going on.

"Are you burning leaves?" he asked.

"No!" said Brother, coughing.

"We are cleaning rugs."

"Here," said Papa. "Let me try."

Papa whacked the rugs.

Even bigger clouds of dust came out.

The dust drifted behind the tree house.

Mama was hanging out her clean wash.

"Oh, my goodness!" said Mama.

"My clean wash is getting dirty!"

She told Papa and the Scouts to stop.

"That's enough rug-beating," she said.

"I have other chores for the Scouts."

Mama sent the Scouts up to the attic.

"There are piles of papers up there,"

said Mama.

"Please tie them up.

Then bring them down to recycle."

The Scouts and Papa went to the attic.

The Scouts tied up the papers.

They knew recycling showed respect

for God's creation.

Papa found some old clothes in a
trunk and put them on.

He put an old record on a record player.

"I remember this old song," Papa said.

He danced around the attic.

Mama heard the music.

She came up to the attic.

"Hello, my dear," said Papa.

"May I have this dance?"

He danced around with Mama.

The Scouts all laughed.

"This is fun," said Mama.

"But chores need to be done."

"You are right," said Papa.

"I will get back to work too."

Papa went back
to his shop.
The Scouts carried the
papers downstairs for
recycling.

"Honey is getting cranky," said Mama.

"Please play with her."

So the Good Deed Scouts

played catch with Honey.

They played peekaboo and blocks.

The Scouts put on a puppet show

for Honey—

"Snow White and the Seven Bears."

Honey giggled and clapped.

Soon it was time for lunch.

Mama made a nice lunch

for the Good Deed Scouts.

"You are the best Mama's helpers

ever!" Mama said.

"Hooray!" said the Scouts.

"Another good deed done!"

"Share your food with hungry people. Provide homeless people with a place to stay."

—Isaiah 58:7

The Berenstain Bears
Help the
Homeless

Story and Pictures By
Jan and Mike Berenstain

Living Lights™

GOOD DEED SCOUTS

ZONDERVAN.com/
AUTHORTRACKER
follow your favorite authors

The Good Deed Scouts were
trying to think of a good deed to do.
Before they could, Widow McBear
came by.

"Hello, scouts," she said.

"I have a good deed for you."

"That's great!" said Brother.

"What is it?" asked Sister.

"I have an old house on top of
Spook Hill," said Widow McBear.
"No one lives there. It is run down."
"It sounds *spooky*!" said Sister to Lizzy.

"I want to make it a home
for the homeless," said Widow McBear.
"Will you scouts fix it up?"
"Yes, we will!" said the Scouts.

"Here is the key," said Widow McBear.

"You can start tonight."

"Tonight?" said Sister.

The scouts were scared.

Sister thought there might be ghosts.

Brother thought there might be goblins.

Lizzy thought there might be monsters.

But Fred was not scared. It was just
an old house. It would make a
good home for the homeless.
"As the Bible says," Fred pointed out,
"'Rescue the weak and the needy.'"
"Good point, Fred," said Brother.

That night the scouts stood
at the bottom of Spook Hill.

"I am afraid there are ghosts," said Sister.

"I am afraid there are goblins," said Brother.

"I am afraid there are monsters," said Lizzy.

"It is just an empty, old house," said Fred.

"Follow me!"

So up Spook Hill the scouts went.

Sister, Brother, and Lizzy were wrong.

There were no ghosts or goblins

or monsters in the house.

But Fred was wrong too.

The house was not empty.
Lots of eyes were looking out of the
windows. Lots of little eyes—
and one pair of big eyes!

The little eyes belonged to the bats
that lived in the house.

The big eyes belonged to Old Tom.

He was a homeless bear.

He stayed at the spooky, old house.

As the scouts came closer,
Old Tom and the bats
grew afraid.

The scouts walked across the porch.

Creak! Creak! went the floor.

Fred turned the doorknob.

Rattle! Rattle! went the knob.

Fred pulled the door open.

Squeeek! went the door.

Bats came flying out the open door!

Whoosh! went the bats.

The scouts went inside.

They saw two big eyes!

"Ghosts!" yelled Sister.

"Goblins!" yelled Brother.

"Monsters!" yelled Lizzy.

"Help!" yelled Old Tom.

"It's Old Tom!" said Brother.

"We see him around town."

"Hello, Tom," said Fred.

"We are the Good Deed Scouts.

We are fixing up this house.

Will you help?"

Old Tom was glad to help.

They started the next day.

They hammered and sawed.

They swept and washed.

They painted and polished.

Soon, the spooky, old house
on top of Spook Hill
looked like new.

Widow McBear came to open the new
Spook Hill Homeless Shelter.
She asked Old Tom to stay and take
care of it. All the homeless bears
of Bear Country came to live there.

The bats stayed too.

They lived up in the attic.

"Thank you for helping the homeless, Good Deed Scouts!" said Widow McBear.

"Thank you for giving us a good deed to do," said Brother.

"As the Bible says," Fred pointed out, "'Learn to do right; seek justice. Defend the oppressed.'"

"Good point, Fred!" they all said.